Best Friends

Shanna Wrazen

The Rosen Publishing Group, Inc.
New York

I read books with my best friend.

I play ball with my best friend.

I fly a kite with my best friend.

I ride bikes with my best friend.

I jump rope with my best friend.

I eat pizza with my best friend.

Words to Know

bikes

friend

kite

pizza

rope